Sound of Her Warrior Heart

a Delta Force romance story
by
M. L. Buchman

Buchman Bookworks

Other works by M.L. Buchman

Roy's Independence Day
Damien's Christmas

AND THE NAVY
Christmas at Steel Beach
Christmas at Peleliu Cove

5E
Target of the Heart
Target Lock on Love
Target of Mine

Delta Force
Target Engaged
Heart Strike

Dead Chef Thrillers
Swap Out!
One Chef!
Two Chef!

Firehawks

MAIN FLIGHT
Pure Heat
Full Blaze
Hot Point
Flash of Fire
Wild Fire

SMOKEJUMPERS
Wildfire at Dawn
Wildfire at Larch Creek
Wildfire on the Skagit

Deities Anonymous

Cookbook from Hell: Reheated
Saviors 101

SF/F Titles
The Nara Reaction
Monk's Maze
the Me and Elsie Chronicles

Strategies for Success: (NF)
Manaaging Your Inner Artist / Writer

Get a free Starter Library at:
www.mlbuchman.com

Don't Miss a Thing!

Sign up for M. L. Buchman's newsletter
today
and receive:
Release News
Free Short Stories
a Free Starter Library

Do it today. Do it now.
http://www.mlbuchman.com/newsletter/

1

Purple.

A purple so deep that it made her think of the purest fresh-pressed grape juice.

Purple grapes. Round globes of color so dark that they ate the brilliant sunlight until they were almost black.

Green leaves. Impossibly blue sky.

Katrina knew something was wrong, but it took her a moment to identify what was missing.

Birds. There should be birdsong. Her family's vineyard was never quiet when the grapes were so close to harvest. This late in the season the bees had moved on to more flowery pastures, but the birds should be singing, arguing, playing.

Funny, she didn't recognize this row of vines, she thought she knew them all.

It was hard to care, though. She'd always loved to lie on the rich soil between the rows of vines and stare at the deeply blue sky. She rarely spent that time thinking about the future or the past. In her memories it hadn't been about some boy either. Of course when the boys came along, she'd spent less time alone in the vineyard watching the sky. No, the vineyard was always about the present moment.

A thread of black smoke slid across the blue sky. Burning a slash pile? To early in the season for that. The summer was still hot and dry.

She reached a hand up through the silence to pluck a grape. They looked ripe enough that half the cluster might fall into her palm at the lightest touch.

Except she didn't recognize the hand. They weren't her slender teenage fingers. Where was the silver thumb ring that Granny had given her at twelve that had finally moved to her middle finger at fourteen?

This hand was strong, with a shooter's callus on the webbing between thumb and forefinger. And why was the hand, *her hand* covered in red, sticky…blood?

A face intervened between her and her view of sky, grape leaves, hand…blood?

It was a hard, male face.

One that needed a shave.

It should have alarmed her that he was so close, but she knew him. Or thought she should.

He wore a close-fitting military helmet and anti-glare glasses. She flexed her jaw and could feel the familiar pressure of the strap of her own helmet. Squinching her nose revealed that she too wore sunglasses.

Why did they need helmets to lie in the vineyard to watch the grapes ripen in the sunshine? She didn't like sunglasses, they changed the color of the blue sky. She tried looking around the edges, but they were wrap-around, just like his.

He was familiar.

Very familiar.

But never from this close. That wasn't normal.

His lips were moving, but she couldn't hear a thing.

"What?"

He clamped a hard hand over her mouth and his lips made a "Shh!" shape, but she couldn't hear anything.

She studied his lips.

Words. They were forming words.

Kat! Are you okay? Not Katrina. Kat wasn't a family nickname. Always her full name in the Melman family. Miss Katrina to the Mexican field hands as if her family were lords and ladies rather than third-generation Oregon vineyard owners.

Sure she was okay. Though it was weird to have the face asking it silently, especially that face. She associated it with a cold, emotionless tone that could slice concrete.

But why wouldn't she be okay? She was lying in a lovely vineyard, the sun warming her face while she watched purple grapes, blue sky, and black smoke from a slash pile fire. It was expanding though. Maybe the fire was out of control.

The bloody hand was still bothering her.

And the silence.

Maybe she wasn't okay.

Maybe she'd been—

The memory slammed in like the blast of a mortar.

Which was exactly what had happened.

2

Sergeant Katrina Melman suddenly remembered the feeling of flying.

There had been the high whistle of an incoming mortar round. She and Tomas—who she always teased about abandoning his poor H somewhere along the way, cruelly leaving it to wander the world on its own—had dropped flat in the vineyard and offered up a quick prayer for the round to land somewhere else.

It had partially worked. Rather than a direct hit, the force of the blast had merely thrown her aside, slamming her into a line of grape vines. The burnt sulfur smell of exploded TNT overwhelmed the sweet grapes and rich soil.

Pain was starting to report in. Abused muscles, the nasty gash on her hand.

Nothing felt broken.

"I think I'm okay."

Tomas shushed her again. Again she had to concentrate on his lips to figure out which words he was speaking silently. *You're shouting.*

"I am?"

Again the hand clamped over her mouth.

The silence. The echoing silence. The world hadn't gone quiet. Her hearing had gone instead.

Deaf.

When she nodded her understanding, Tomas eased off his hold on her. He mouthed out some long sentence that she had no hope of unraveling, especially as he kept looking away to scan the vineyard, hiding his mouth in the process.

"I can't hear you," she tried to make it a whisper.

Tomas spun back to face her and winced.

Unable to hear herself, she'd lost all calibration of her volume.

You can't? Tomas' lips moved, but she heard nothing—not even the proverbial pin. At least she was fairly sure that's what he'd said. Lipreading was something they taught undercover types. She was a shooter.

Katrina stuck with just shaking her head.

Shit! No problem reading that. With quick rough hands he began inspecting her.

She slapped his hands aside then sat up, and wished she hadn't. Every muscle screamed— silently—in protest. She began inspecting herself. Everything moved when she tried it. A quick pat-down revealed no sources of blood other than her hand.

Tomas bound that quickly enough, using the medkit that hung from his vest.

Armored vest.

Field.

Mortar.

She looked around and spotted her rifle tangled in one of the grapevines. She slid it out and it appeared none the worse for having been blown up.

"That makes one of us who's okay," she whispered to her baby. The MK21 Precision Sniper Rifle was fifty-two inches and eighteen pounds of silent death that let her "reach out and touch someone" over a mile away. It was her reason for being—her role in Delta Force. Her role in—

Moldova. She and her rifle had been blown up in a vineyard in the Eastern European country sandwiched between Ukraine and Romania. Except no one was supposed to know they were here. They—

Tomas slammed her down to the ground and lay on top of her and her rifle. She could feel by the rigidity of his body that he wasn't dead. He was bracing over her like a human shield. For half a moment she thought she finally saw a bird flying across the sky. A falcon swooping on its prey. An…incoming round!

She felt the ground buck against her back from the explosion. The air blast hit against the far side of the vines, peppering the two of them with hundreds of grapes blown off the vines. The vintner was going to be furious.

Tomas pushed back to kneeling beside her.

We've… but Tomas turned away and she missed the rest of his sentence. It was as if he didn't want to look at her after lying full length upon her a moment before. They were both wearing combat vests, making it one of the unsexiest moments ever, but she got the feeling he was still embarrassed by it.

Sitting up, she grabbed the helmet straps on either side of his jaw and turned him back to face her.

"What did you say?" Katrina struggled to keep it soft. Tomas didn't reprimand her so she must have succeeded. "I'm deaf."

His eyes widened briefly. Then he grabbed her head, his powerful hands strong but gentle along her cheeks, and turned it to either side to inspect her ears.

No blood, his lips formed the words quickly, but she hoped she got it right.

She heaved out a sigh of relief at his words. Good. That was good. No dribbling blood meant that maybe her eardrums were still intact.

He made a sharp slicing motion to the west with a flat hand. Right. They needed to get moving. He signaled reminders to stay low and go down the center of the path—jostling a vine might give away their changing position.

At her nod, he led off.

Stepping out, she walked straight into a grapevine.

She scooted to the middle of the path and tried again.

This time she plunged into the grapes the next row over.

It wasn't vertigo, she'd had that induced during training and learned how to fire through it. Besides, vertigo always made you spin in the same direction. With her ears out of operation, her balance was off.

Tomas grabbed her arm and, though it felt like he was pulling her hard to the right, they progressed straight down the aisle of dirt between two rows of green leaves with her weaving like a drunkard.

Fifteen seconds later she felt the air thump against her back as a mortar killed the poor grapevines she'd stumbled into. Whoever was firing at them was good.

3

By the end of the row, she began to get a feel for how to counteract her balance problems.

Tomas yanked her down to the soil, scanning the terrain ahead. He might be a hardcore pain in the ass, but she couldn't ask for a better soldier to be at her side. There was no better man to be in a tight situation with in Delta.

She'd tried to talk to him in camp, but he always gave her the cold shoulder, with a voice that could be used to chill a meat locker.

However, on assignment, he guarded her like a mother hen or big brother.

He was the best soldier, and she'd always been drawn to the best, but for some reason he wouldn't even give her the time of day once they were back in a green zone.

That green zone felt awfully far away at the moment.

They lay together at the edge of the lush vineyard. Looking back she could see that it swooped down into a valley and up the next hill in neat and orderly rows. She'd never had a Moldovan wine and wondered if they were any good. Simply by the size of the field, they were successful. She plucked a grape. Blue-purple. Thick skin that resisted her bite before it popped, flooding her mouth with a high sugar content. Merlot probably. Or maybe a Zinfandel, they tasted a lot alike while still in the grape. She could be lying in the hills of Oregon's Willamette Valley…if it weren't for someone firing a mortar at them. Very few mortars being fired in the Willamette Valley in her experience.

Right! Time to start thinking like a soldier again.

Ahead lay a five-meter strip of rough dirt thick with tractor tire tracks. Beyond it lay a field of thin brown stalks chopped off at one meter high. It was a no-man's land in which they'd be completely exposed. Past several hundred meters of stalks, a line of trees.

Tomas tapped her arm and pointed to the right.

Katrina had to scoot forward to see around him. A large red combine was parked in the middle of the field, at the edge of the tall stubble. Beyond it stood sunflowers—acres of sunflowers. Their heads were dried to a gray-brown and the combine would soon be harvesting them. Except the cab was empty and the door hung open. The machine still vibrated and smoke swirled up out of its exhaust stack. The farmer had abandoned his vehicle when the shelling had started.

"I hate working with foreign military."

Tomas nodded his agreement.

That's what must have happened. Moldova was way down the list on the international index of governmental corruption—their score was in the bottom third and falling fast. You could buy the entire parliament for the price of a Super Bowl commercial. Throw in a signed football and you could probably buy the military as well. The US must have dutifully informed someone of their planned operation on Moldovan soil, who had then reported it directly to the Russians who coveted Moldovan territory. Or perhaps she and Tomas were still alive because some faction of the local military had decided to take care of the problem themselves—it wasn't like the Russians to miss quite so many times.

Well, killing a pair of Delta Force operators wasn't all that easy either.

"Where are they?" she asked Tomas quietly. There were two scenarios: the people firing the mortar could see their position, or the mortar crew were hunkered down, out of sight, but had a spotter who could. Either way she and Tomas had to find them.

Tomas pulled out a small radio scanner. In

moments he had a lock on the enemy's frequency. She could see by the indicator light that they were real talkers, either locals or overconfident Russians. He hooked up a small DF loop and began rotating it to get their direction.

She tried to remember how she'd been lying on the ground when she'd seen the incoming round. It had come from…the line of trees to the west.

Tomas pointed in two places: one toward the trees, one…in the direction of the combine.

Katrina slid the caps off the ends of her rifle's scope. She tapped Tomas' shoulder. He turned to her and she made as if to press her hand flat against the ground, then repeated the motion on his shoulder.

He lay flat, braced his elbows wide so that he was steadier than the Rock of Gibraltar. Then he rested his head on his folded hands, but turned toward her rather than the combine. Dark eyes. She could feel his dark eyes watching her despite the lenses he wore. They have always watched her, the sole woman on their squad. Every time she turned, Tomas' eyes were tracking her.

Ignoring that, she unfolded the bipod on the front of her weapon and rested it against the small of his back. The combine was parked a thousand meters away and upslope from them so she needed the extra height to brace her weapon. She lined up with a break in the vines and began inspecting the combine at high magnification.

The main harvester bar was set a meter high

and she could see its cutters still working. The high cab was indeed empty. The unloading pipe was swung back out of the way. The…

She swung back to inspect the cab. It was empty. But through the double layer of glass, windshield and side window, she could just make out a man standing behind the cab. It was an almost impossible shot, especially for a single shooter. She would have to break the windshield, then the side window, and then might have a chance of hitting the target if he hadn't already moved. Two shots minimum, probably three.

Tracking upward, seeking any way in, she spotted just what she needed. Between the top of the cab and some other piece of gear, a pair of binoculars inspected the vineyard. She flipped off the safety, glanced at the grapevines to estimate the wind—it was so strange not to hear it rustling the leaves—and compensated for the bullet's fall and a thousand meters of windage.

The MK21 had a silencer, but there was always some noise. Now, for her, it was truly silent as it kicked her in the shoulder. A half second later, the binoculars were gone. Between the combine's tires she could see a body plummet onto the field. She worked the bolt and fed another round into the downed spotter just to be sure, not that a .338 Lapua Magnum round would have left much of his head. Even at over a half-mile out, the body twitched from the massive kinetic impact of the bullet. No question that the spotter for the mortar team was permanently out of commission.

There was a whiff of burnt gunpowder as she chambered another round.

She glanced at Tomas and nodded that it was done, but froze halfway through.

He was smiling at her. It was gone the moment she'd caught him at it, but she knew she'd seen it. Tomas didn't smile at anybody for any reason.

No. That wasn't right. She'd seen his smile before—never directed at her, of course—but she'd seen it. But his face, when he smiled, made it possible to imagine Tomas speaking to her in a warm and gentle tone. *That* was too strange for words so she kept her silence.

4

Clearing out the mortar team didn't take long. Idiot One sprang up to go check on the shooter. Idiot Two raced away in plain view and earned himself a shot in the back though he was closer to a mile away by the time Tomas pointed him out.

Katrina busted up the mortar tube and defused the remaining ammo while Tomas hid the bodies. He showed her the spotter's arm tattoo—a black bat hovering over a blue circle meant to represent the Earth. It was a Spetsnaz tat, Russian Special Forces. So, their enemies this morning were one Russian and two locals, because a Spetsnaz would never run from a fight. Spetsnaz. It was a surprise that she and Tomas survived. Definitely time to go.

Her feet were now steady enough that she probably could have navigated on her own, but

Tomas showed no inclination to let go of his grip on her upper arm and she wasn't complaining.

There was a steadiness to him. Not merely his gait, but his reliability. His grip never varied, except to tighten briefly when she stumbled on a particularly gnarly root. He scanned ahead as they moved through the woods.

Last night's insertion into Moldova had been screwed up in a bazillion different ways. The mortar attack counted as a bazillion-and-one.

First, the transport helo had a mechanical failure. A team of mechanics had raced to fix it deep into the night. So, their launch window at dusk had, well, gone out the window. They'd finally hit the ground in eastern Moldova at two a.m. But their ride had long since given up and vanished into the darkness. No option left but to cover the ground on foot, dressed in full US military gear, with much of the transit in broad daylight.

That's why they'd ducked into the vineyard in the first place, good cover. Into a vineyard—and straight into a trap.

Tomas set a ground-eating pace through the woods that they could both maintain for hours with only minimal breaks. Once they were deep in the woods and several kilometers from the dead mortar team, they made quick work of cutting down some wild cherry branches and creating a small lean-to using the massive trunk of a fallen oak. It was several feet larger around than the Willamette oaks, it must be an English oak. She'd always wanted to go walking among the Cotswolds of England and see some of them. Now she was being hunted across the Moldovan countryside. It sure wasn't the same.

Inside their shelter, Tomas called up to Command during a satellite overflight. She couldn't lipread a word because he held the radio so close to his mouth. Whatever their conversation was, it was short.

Katrina focused on picking the small wild cherries off the roof of their bower for them to eat. Tart! But good.

That's when the fact of her deafness slammed home and stole her breath away. What if it wasn't temporary? At first she hadn't had time to think about it, then she'd shoved aside her fear by convincing herself it was just a TTS, a temporary threshold shift. But what if it wasn't? What if—

Tomas tapped her on the shoulder and she almost cried out in shock.

He eyed her carefully, making a point to mouth his question slowly, *You okay?*

So not. But she gave him a nod that was a total lie.

He snapped his fingers close by her ears.

She could only shake her head.

In answer, Tomas reached out and pulled her against his chest. It was awkward; all of the gear on their vests kept it from being close and she had a fistful of cherries, but still she appreciated it. For a moment she lay her cheek against the cool metal of the emergency lifting ring on the front of his vest, and let herself be held.

Making sense of that was no easier than making sense of her deafness.

A woman in Delta Force did *not* let herself be held. She didn't dare let herself be seen as weak, not for a millisecond. Women were too rare a breed in Special Operations and especially in the heavy-duty combat units.

Beyond that, the last person on the planet she'd ever expect to have empathy was Sergeant Tomas Gallagher—the toughest damn bastard in anyone's army. It was easy to remember his cold, hard voice. But she couldn't reconcile that with the way he was taking care of her.

He held her until she felt some sense of control come back. Not relief. Not hope. But at least the sense that somehow or other she'd get through this and that maybe, just maybe, she wasn't going to be alone in that effort.

She sat up and patted his arm in thanks. It was a good arm, thick with muscle, honed with thousands of hours of training and hundreds of missions. She realized she needed to make herself stop patting him.

Distraction needed.

Katrina passed him a handful of the tart cherries after making clear he had to spit out the cherry pits—they were naturally laced with cyanide. Then she pointed at the sky, to where the satellite antenna had been aimed and made a questioning face.

You can talk, Tomas admonished her. *Soft-ly.* He was over-accentuating his lip movement which helped. Tomas Gallagher being thoughtful was still a shock.

She shrugged at her descent into sign language. Not being able to hear immersed her into a strange world of silence that she felt reluctant to break. Also, her own voice was wrong—foreign, muted to silence by whatever was happening in her ears. She could feel that she was speaking, but couldn't hear it, neither volume nor tone.

He tapped the lapel of his shirt, pointed again to the west, tapped his watch, and gave a thumbs up. Command had reported that their targets, a Russian general and a Moldovan one, were still expected to be in position at the time previously reported.

Good news. The mission wasn't blown yet despite the problems they'd encountered.

He pointed upward, held up three fingers, then placed his hands palm to palm against his own cheek before closing his eyes.

She didn't get it.

He began slapping his pockets but pencil and paper weren't something you carried on a self-contained mission into a "friendly" foreign country. He looked around again, then spotted something.

He held his hand palm up and moved it until he was almost touching her breast. He did it fast enough that she jolted back against the log.

Tomas held up a hand in apology and, if she didn't know better, she'd say he blushed.

This time he moved his palm more slowly until it was suddenly filled with the bright light of a sunbeam that had found its way down through the forest canopy and into their hastily assembled hideout. It had been shining against her ribcage. He tapped his palm, then pointed upward.

"Oh, the sun."

He nodded. This time the three fingers, a tap of his watch, and a sign to sleep made sense. Three hours to sunset when it would be time to move out; she *should* get some sleep.

Tapping his own chest, he made the signal for lookout—a hand shading his eyes.

She held up two fingers, then bent one in half.

Oh, she could speak.

"Hour and a half, then it's my turn to watch."

He nodded and she settled herself more comfortably against the log. A Special Ops soldier could sleep anywhere: a roaring plane flight, inside a bunker during a firefight—didn't matter. Their small shelter was cozy. It smelled of fresh cherries that matched the vivid taste on her tongue and crispy-dry oak leaves. And was very, very quiet.

She sighed.

Then she remembered what it had felt like to be held by Tomas. They were shoulder to shoulder. He had good shoulders.

After a night and a day on the go, she was exhausted.

She leaned her head onto his shoulder and felt him jolt in surprise. It was a long time before his arm settled as lightly as the sunlight on her shoulders. She didn't stay awake long enough to feel whether or not his fingers wrapped around her arm.

5

Katrina awoke with a start. It was soft twilight. She listened carefully, but didn't hear a thing… because, shit, she was deaf. This was definitely going to take some getting used to.

She was also warm and comfortable inside the curve of a man's arm. Of Tomas Gallagher's arm. For a moment she let herself revel in the feel of it, the security of being held, of lying against a man she trusted with her very life.

Except they were both soldiers.

As she pushed herself upright, he eased his arm off her shoulders.

"You didn't wake me for my half of the watch."

He shrugged.

She thumped the side of a fist against his shoulder.

He tapped his ear and then hers with a soft touch.

Oh right, she couldn't listen. "Sorry. I hope you didn't mind me sleeping on you."

He clamped both hands around his own throat and pretended he was gagging.

She clamped a hand over her mouth to suppress the laugh and wondered where the hell Sergeant Tomas Gallagher had gone. The man she knew had absolutely no sense of humor.

"You're being nice to me."

He shrugged and looked down to rummage through his kit for some energy bars. She didn't take the one he offered.

"Why?"

He turned away but stopped when she rested a palm on his cheek. Without his sunglasses, his dark eyes bored into hers. She tried to say something, she truly did, but her throat was suddenly dry.

"Why, Tomas?" finally creaked out of her throat.

He rested one of his big hands over where hers still touched his cheek.

The light was making it harder to see, but he might have said, *I'm an idiot.*

A moment later he leaned forward and kissed her. It wasn't some tentative little peck. It wasn't a question either. It was a kiss that demanded attention. It was hard, fast, and deep. He grabbed either side of her armored vest by the armholes and hauled her into his lap.

Tomas' strength was overwhelming, pinning her against him.

She knew that at the least hesitation on her part, he'd let her go, but no hesitation came from anywhere inside her.

Surprise? *Hell yeah!*

Hesitation? *Hell no!* Not from a kiss like the one he was delivering.

In the same unit? *Don't give a shit!*

On a mission? The mission could wait just a goddamn minute—she was busy here. Busy having her rocketing heartrate pound against her chest, if not her ears.

He let her go at last and some small bit of her sanity returned. She was straddling his lap, her arms locked around his neck. One of his hands had slipped down between her armor and butt.

And he was grinning like the big bad wolf.

"You're not a bit sorry, are you?"

He patted his free hand downward to remind her to watch her voice. His other hand was still occupied elsewhere. He shook his head.

"Odd. Neither am I."

She couldn't hear his groan, but she could feel it conducting through her fingertips. He said something that she couldn't begin to follow, especially with the last of the light.

Katrina could only shrug.

He dug his fingers hard into her bottom one last time, pulling her tight against him, vest to vest.

Yep! Her body was screaming for it too, but…

"Mission time," she kept it soft.

He nodded and they tried to disentangle themselves. Somehow one of her pockets of .338 Lapua Magnum magazines got hooked on his spare 7.62mm magazines for the HK416 combat rifle he carried and it took them a moment to move apart.

Once separated, she became terribly self conscious. They *were* on a mission. They *were* in the same squad. And Tomas Gallagher hated having a woman in The Unit—that much she was sure of. Except now she wasn't.

Had he been avoiding her for other reasons than she'd thought?

Duh! So if *why* wasn't the right question, the next question was…"How long?" She tapped his chest then hers to make it clear what she was asking.

He held up a single finger.

"One hour? One day?"

He made a flipping motion.

"Day One?"

He nodded.

"You wanted to kiss me since the first day I joined The Unit? Why?" *Now* "why" was the right question.

He rolled his eyes at her. He tapped her on the chest and held up a single finger again.

"Because I'm the only woman on the team?"

No. He tapped her chest—directly on the sniper rifle magazines that had just tangled them up. Then on the MK21 before he tried a double thumbs up. *You best. Very sexy,* he mouthed carefully. He ran his hand down her vest's side plates, over her ribs, waist, and hips to make his point.

"Because I shoot well? That's exactly what every woman wants to be admired for," despite her words it *did* mean a lot.

In answer he ran a knuckle over her cheek so gently that she couldn't help closing her eyes.

"Okay, not just because I shoot well."

He nodded with a grin. Then he dug out his night-vision goggles and clipped them onto his helmet.

"You are a mystery to me, Mr. Tomas Gallagher."

He gave her a thumbs up and another one of those killer smiles once she had her own NVGs in place and turned on.

6

Seven hours hard hiking to reach their target point and three more hours to investigate possible hides.

Command had, of course, done their usual head game. That told them that the CIA was calling the shots on this one because they never did anything straightforward if they could do it bass-ackwards instead.

Katrina decided that it was a good thing she'd been in the Army for long enough to know that they *always* did that. At least it made it so that she was only royally pissed rather than in a murderous rage when the truth came out.

When Tomas reported that they were on site, Command informed them that it was the *Moldovan* general who was their target. He was the only person who'd been told about their mission at all. The fact that they'd been attacked by Russian Special Forces had served to confirm that he could be easily bought.

The Moldovan prime minister himself had told his general that the secrecy of this operation was a matter of Moldovan National Security. Yet here that general was, meeting with a Russian general at a base just over the Moldovan border in Transnistria.

Transnistria was a breakaway region of Moldova, aligned with the Russians rather than the US, NATO, and the EU. Only four other nations recognized it, though it had been a splinter nation since 1992. A splinter the Russians wanted to exploit. Re-annexing Moldova, just as they had the Crimea, would help secure the Russian frontier against an attack by land forces.

Nobody in the West was in favor of that, except the purchased general. The prime minister of Moldova couldn't be seen to act against his own military despite his general's other war crimes, but it was time for a message to be sent.

And apparently it was up to her and Tomas to send it.

As part of the plan, she'd brought a second barrel and bolt for her rifle, and ammunition to match. In less than two minutes she'd changed from the far-reaching hammer of .338 Lapua to an odd cartridge only ever used in Russia, a 5.45x39mm. It fired only half the distance forcing them to find a location that was both well hidden and close to the meeting site.

Tiraspol airport was technically non-operational, despite being the only airport in the splinter country and housing all five planes of their air force. No one was sure if they could fly, or survive taking off on the aged runway even if they did work.

But helicopters could land here just fine.

It was finding suitable cover that was the issue. They had to get close, preferably well under five hundred meters with such small caliber ammunition, and yet not be found after she took the shot.

Tomas led her in. The airport was unlit except for a single streetlight near the entrance. The runway itself was open to the surrounding farmland, making it easy to walk onto the airfield. They lay in the unmown grass at one end of the runway and inspected the structures carefully.

He tapped his radio, then pointed at the only decent building left standing.

"Command says that's where the meeting will be?"

Tomas nodded.

She studied it through her rifle's night scope and shook her head. Not a chance from here.

Tomas grinned and tapped his temple.

Katrina gestured for him to lead on.

Sticking to a dry drainage ditch behind the buildings, they crossed behind the old terminal and slipped up to the remains of the Transnistrian Air Force. Five Antonov transport planes, all with flat tires—none operational. A dozen helicopters, only two of which looked serviceable, and a pair of Yak two-seat trainers that must date back to World War II. One was clearly being scrapped for parts, but the other one looked serviceable. It was long, an olive-drab green, and had one of those humped glass canopies.

She shook her head.

He tapped the side of the plane.

She shook her head again.

Tomas pointed at the office building.

Three hundred meters away, an ideal shot.

"This is your idea of an exfiltration plan after we're done here? An ancient airplane that may not fly? I'd like to survive this mission."

In answer, he leaned in and kissed her lightly. Apparently he wanted to survive it as well. How was she supposed to argue with how his lightest touch could make her feel?

7

Katrina awaited her moment. She was slouched in the front seat of the Yak-18. It smelled of old pilot sweat, gasoline, and sausages. At the moment she was not appreciating her heightened awareness of her sense of smell since going deaf.

Tomas—presently in the pilot's seat behind her—had inspected and prepped the plane, encouraged at finding the gas tanks full. Then they'd nudged the tail around until she had a perfect shot through the partially open canopy. There would be no sign of where the shot had come from. No one would look in the middle of the airfield. And if someone did, Tomas was confident he could get the plane moving quickly.

The meeting happened as planned. At noon, a brand-new Kamov Ka-62 Executive transport helicopter flew in and landed exactly where expected. It was met within minutes by two cars that had swept in through the front gate.

Tomas knew that if he needed her attention, he could thump a fist on the side of the airframe from his position in the rear pilot's seat well behind her. But for now, her attention was narrowing. It was Tomas' job to make sure that she stayed safe. It was her job to erase the man who had set a trap for her and betrayed his prime minister.

She couldn't kill the Moldovan general outright, or they'd know there was a sniper on the field, but she had a plan.

First to emerge were a half-dozen guards from either side. Then the two generals climbed out of their respective craft at the same moment and approached each other. A Transnistrian official, also resplendent in his uniform, accompanied the Moldovan. It was too perfect.

The guards formed a wide circle facing outwards, thankfully none quite facing their aircraft—even with the flash suppressor, her shot would not be invisible.

The windsock was rippling hard, ten mile-an-hour crosswind, gusting to twenty. Thankfully, she had fired a few thousand rounds of the 5.45mm ammunition at the Fort Bragg firing range to familiarize herself with its flight characteristics— the wind was going to drag this round a long way sideways in three hundred meters. It would make her shot look as if it was coming from well to the west of their current position if someone noticed the angle of attack.

The two generals approached one another, with the Moldovan facing her but not yet blocked by the Russian.

Three shots. If she was shooting as a Delta, she'd use four, but the Russians fought differently.

When they were two steps apart, she fired a single round into the Moldovan general's heart. Delta would have placed two there.

On her next heartbeat—in his face. It caught him before he was over the surprise of the first shot.

For the last shot, she picked a Russian guard standing behind the Russian general and put a round through the meat of his thigh.

At his scream, the Russian general yanked out his sidearm as he spun. He then shot the first Transnistrian guard he spotted. In moments, all of the Transnitrian locals were gunned down—including the high-ranking official.

Someone must have forewarned the police—at least enough so as to make them station a team nearby. They swarmed out of the office building and had the Russian general, his troops, and the helicopter pilot under arrest within moments.

Katrina eased her weapon back in through the plane's canopy and waited, but no one so much as looked in their direction. Who would attack from the middle of their own airfield when the perpetrator was so obviously caught red-handed?

The Russians were going to have very poor relations with Transnistria for some time to come. And Delta? They'd never been here at all.

8

"Can't we just walk out?" Katrina waved past the canopy at the deserted airfield. Darkness had come and shrouded the only signs of what had happened today: bloodstains on the sun-bleached pavement and an abandoned Russian helicopter.

It was awkward, twisting in her seat to see Tomas' lips with her NVGs. He said something that she couldn't follow.

"What?"

Trust me, accompanied by one of his smiles. She'd learned about them. They were full of promises—ones that she hoped, no, that she *knew* he would keep. It made him impossible to argue with. She just wished that she could imagine his voice as anything other than harsh and cold, but it was all she'd ever heard from him.

She turned back in her seat and tightened the cross-shoulder harness.

"Why walk when you can fly?" She finally worked out that was what he'd said.

She'd had the mandatory basic training and could survive as pilot in a half-dozen different aircraft—*survive*. Her only hope was that his skills were far more practiced than her own. Thankfully, the Yah-18 was a trainer: pilot in the rear, student in the front. It meant she didn't have to touch anything.

No one bothered them as the engine caught and spun to life on the darkened airfield. It shook the plane, momentarily filling the cabin with the acrid bite of exhaust fumes but, at least to her, it was painfully silent.

Tomas taxied them to the blacked-out runway. Then, unleashing a mighty vibration that she assumed was accompanied by a massive roar, the single engine awoke and pulled them down the abandoned runway. The plane jounced and wobbled, but they were aloft before it could shatter her spine.

Once in the air, Tomas turned them south with a confidence she knew she lacked. Safe in his care. Safe in his arms.

The irony wasn't lost on her for a moment. Tomas' very careful attempts to not treat her differently, to not show her his feelings, had only served to enhance them.

She now understood his prior silences. And

those in turn had made her more aware of him. It had made her notice what a standout soldier he was. And their distance had probably driven him even harder to excel, which had only made her notice him all the more.

Yet she'd already been deaf the first time he demonstrated his feelings. Even if the damage was permanent, there was no questioning the truth of them—not of the man who had thrown himself over her so that the mortar might somehow kill him but spare her, and not of the man who now flew the old Yak from close behind her.

A half hour later, they slid out of the sky and landed on a long sandy beach. The plane jolted, but not too badly. As always, Tomas knew exactly what he was doing.

They sat together on the sandy shore of a Romanian park along the Black Sea. Small waves broke on the sand in clean white lines as they watched the night together. Tomas had radioed for a helicopter from an American helicopter carrier that was cruising offshore. It would pick them up soon—and drag the old plane out to sink in the depths of the Black Sea erasing the last evidence of anyone interfering at Tiraspol. Now it would just be a plane gone missing on a much more news-worthy day.

They sat close, hip to hip on the sand.

"What if my hearing doesn't come back?" Their NVGs were pushed back on their helmets, so she might as well have been talking to herself.

She wouldn't be able to read any reply on his lips.

But she wasn't alone. He pulled her tight against his side and kissed her on the temple.

Not alone.

She'd always been alone. The family's black sheep, the first one *ever* to enter military service. One of the first women to qualify for front-line combat. Again one of the first into Delta Force. Delta had accepted her, even welcomed her, but she'd been the only woman on her team. It was a lonely existence.

Tomas continued to hold her close. Rather than going for the kiss, that she would have gladly welcomed, he somehow knew she needed something else even more. Instead, he just held her.

The fear began to slide away.

The fear of the mission—always there during but already fading fast, as usual.

The fear of not being good enough to be a woman in Delta. Even if it was her final mission today, she'd proven that she belonged.

The unrealized terror that she'd always be an outsider, always alone. All she had to do was breathe in the warm, earthy, and slightly sweet smell of Tomas Gallagher that reminded her of lying in a vineyard beneath the ripening grapes.

One fear remained. A fear worse than never hearing again. A fear that—

Then she became aware of something. It was

so foreign that she couldn't make sense of it for a moment. It had been going on for a while.

"Hey!"

She could feel Tomas twist to look at where she lay tucked inside the curve of his arm.

"I can hear the waves on the sand." Whatever her body had done to protect her during the explosion had released its hold on her hearing.

"Really?" Now she would forever know what his voice could sound like—soft, kind, and filled with wonder.

"Really." And then her last fear slid into the night. The fear that she'd never get to hear Tomas Gallagher say, "I love you."

About the Author

M.L. Buchman started the first of, what is now over 50 novels and as many short stories, while flying from South Korea to ride his bicycle across the Australian Outback. Part of a solo around the world trip that ultimately launched his writing career.

All three of his military romantic suspense series—The Night Stalkers, Firehawks, and Delta Force—have had a title named "Top 10 Romance of the Year" by the American Library Association's Booklist. NPR and Barnes & Noble have named other titles "Top 5 Romance of the Year." In 2016 he was a finalist for Romance Writers of America prestigious RITA award. He also writes: contemporary romance, thrillers, and fantasy.

Past lives include: years as a project manager,

rebuilding and single-handing a fifty-foot sailboat, both flying and jumping out of airplanes, and he has designed and built two houses. He is now making his living as a full-time writer on the Oregon Coast with his beloved wife and is constantly amazed at what you can do with a degree in Geophysics. You may keep up with his writing and receive a free starter e-library by subscribing to his newsletter at:

www.mlbuchman.com

If you enjoyed this story, you might also enjoy:

Target of the Heart (excerpt)
-a Night Stalkers 5E novel-

Major Pete Napier hovered his MH-47G Chinook helicopter ten kilometers outside of Lhasa, Tibet and a mere two inches off the tundra. A mixed action team of Delta Force and The Activity—the slipperiest intel group on the planet—flung themselves aboard.

The additional load sent an infinitesimal shift in the cyclic control in his right hand. The hydraulics to close the rear loading ramp hummed through the entire frame of the massive helicopter. By the time his crew chief could reach forward to slap an "all secure" signal against his shoulder, they were already ten feet up and fifty out. That was enough altitude. He kept the nose down as he clawed for speed in the thin air at eleven thousand feet.

"Totally worth it," one of the D-boys announced as soon as he was on the Chinook's internal intercom.

He'd have to remember to tell that to the two Black Hawks flying guard for him…when they were in a friendly country and could risk a radio transmission. This deep inside China—or rather Chinese-held territory as the CIA's mission-briefing spook had insisted on calling it—radios attracted attention and were only used to avoid imminent death and destruction.

"Great, now I just need to get us out of this alive."

"Do that, Pete. We'd appreciate it."

He wished to hell he had a stealth bird like the one that had gone into bin Laden's compound. But the one that had crashed during that raid had been blown up. Where there was one, there were always two, but the second had gone back into hiding as thoroughly as if it had never existed. He hadn't heard a word about it since.

The Tibetan terrain was amazing, even if all

he could see of it was the monochromatic green of night vision. And blackness. The largest city in Tibet lay a mere ten kilometers away and they were flying over barren wilderness. He could crash out here and no one would know for decades unless some yak herder stumbled upon them. Or were yaks in Mongolia? He was a corn-fed, white boy from Colorado, what did he know about Tibet? Most of the countries he'd flown into on black ops missions he'd only seen at night anyway.

While moving very, very fast.

Like now.

The inside of his visor was painted with over-lapping readouts. A pre-defined terrain map, the best that modern satellite imaging could build made the first layer. This wasn't some crappy, on-line, look-at-a-picture-of-your-house display. Someone had a pile of dung outside their goat pen? He could see it, tell you how high it was, and probably say if they were pygmy goats or full-size LaManchas by the size of their shit-pellets if he zoomed in.

On top of that were projected the forward-looking infrared camera images. The FLIR imaging gave him a real-time overlay, in case someone had put an addition onto their goat shed since the last satellite pass, or parked their tractor across his intended flight path.

His nervous system was paying autonomic attention to that combined landscape. He also compensated for the thin air at altitude as he instinctively chose when to start his climb over said goat shed or his swerve around it.

It was the third layer, the tactical display that had most of his attention. At least he and the two Black Hawks flying escort on him were finally on the move.

To insert this deep into Tibet, without passing over Bhutan or Nepal, they'd had to add wingtanks on the Black Hawks' hardpoints where he'd much rather have a couple banks of Hellfire missiles. Still, they had 20mm chain guns and the crew chiefs had miniguns which was some comfort.

While the action team was busy infiltrating the capital city and gathering intelligence on the particularly brutal Chinese assistant administrator, he and his crews had been squatting out in the wilderness under a camouflage net designed to make his helo look like just another god-forsaken Himalayan lump of granite.

Command had determined that it was better for the helos to wait on site through the day than risk flying out and back in. He and his crew had stood shifts on guard duty, but none of them had slept. They'd been flying together too long to have any new jokes, so they'd played a lot of cribbage. He'd long ago ruled no gambling on a mission, after a fistfight had broken out about a bluff hand that cost a Marine three hundred and forty-seven dollars. Marines hated losing to Army no matter how many times it happened. They'd had to sit on him for a long time before he calmed down.

Tonight's mission was part of an on-going campaign to discredit the Chinese "presence" in Tibet on the international stage—as if occupying the country the last sixty years didn't count toward ruling, whether invited or not. As usual, there was a crucial vote coming up at the U.N.—that, as usual, the Chinese could be guaranteed to ignore. However, the ever-hopeful CIA was in a hurry to make sure that any damaging information that they could validate was disseminated as thoroughly as possible prior to the vote.

Not his concern.

His concern was, were they going to pass over some Chinese sentry post at their top speed of a hundred and ninety-six miles an hour? The sentries would then call down a couple Shenyang J-16 jet fighters that could hustle along at Mach 2 to fry his sorry ass. He knew there was a pair of them parked at Lhasa along with some older gear that would be just as effective against his three helos.

"Don't suppose you could get a move on, Pete?"

"Eat shit, Nicolai!" He was a good man to have as a copilot. Pete knew he was holding on too tight, and Nicolai knew that a joke was the right way to ease the moment.

He, Nicolai, and the four pilots in the two

Black Hawks had a long way to go tonight and he'd never make it if he stayed so tight on the controls that he could barely maneuver. Pete eased off and felt his fingers tingle with the rush of returning blood. They dove down into gorges and followed them as long as they dared. They hugged cliff walls at every opportunity to decrease their radar profile. And they climbed.

That was the true danger—they would be up near the helos' limits when they crossed over the backbone of the Himalayas in their rush for India. The air was so rarefied that they burned fuel at a prodigious rate. Their reserve didn't allow for any extended battles while crossing the border…not for any battle at all really.

# # #

It was pitch dark outside her helicopter when Captain Danielle Delacroix stamped on the left rudder pedal while giving the big Chinook right-directed control on the cyclic. It tipped her most of the way onto her side, but let her continue in a straight line. A Chinook's rotors were sixty feet across—front to back they overlapped to make the spread a hundred feet long. By cross-controlling her bird to tip it, she managed to execute a straight line between two mock pylons only thirty feet apart. They were made of thin cloth so they wouldn't down the helo if you sliced one—she was the only trainee to not have cut one yet.

At her current angle of attack, she took up less

than a half-rotor of width, just twenty-four feet. That left her nearly three feet to either side, sufficient as she was moving at under a hundred knots.

The training instructor sitting beside her in the copilot's seat didn't react as she swooped through the training course at Fort Campbell, Kentucky. Only child of a single mother, she was used to providing her own feedback loops, so she didn't expect anything else. Those who expected outside validation rarely survived the SOAR induction testing, never mind the two years of training that followed.

As a loner kid, Danielle had learned that self-motivated congratulations and fun were much easier to come by than external ones. She'd spent innumerable hours deep in her mind as a pre-teen superheroine. At twenty-nine she was well on her way to becoming a real life one, though Helo-girl had never been a character she'd thought of in her youth.

External validation or not, after two years of training with the U.S. Army's 160th Special Operations Aviation Regiment she was ready for some action. At least *she* was convinced that she was. But the trainers of Fort Campbell, Kentucky had not signed off on anyone in her trainee class yet. Nor had they given any hint of when they might.

She ducked ten tons of racing Chinook under a bridge and bounced into a near vertical climb to clear the power line on the far side. Like a ride on the toboggan at Terrassee Dufferin during Le Carnaval de Québec, only with five thousand horsepower at her fingertips. Using her Army signing bonus—the first money in her life that was truly hers—to attend *Le Carnaval* had been her one trip back to her birthplace since her mother took them to America when she was ten.

To even apply to SOAR required five years of prior military rotorcraft experience. She had applied after seven years because of a chance encounter—or rather what she'd thought was a chance encounter at the time.

Captain Justin Roberts had been a top Chinook pilot, the one who had convinced her to switch from her beloved Black Hawk and try out the massive twin-rotor craft. One flight and she'd been a goner, begging her commander until he gave in and let her cross over to the new platform. Justin had made the jump from the 10th Mountain Division to the 160th SOAR not long after that.

Then one night she'd been having pizza in Watertown, New York a couple miles off the 10th's base at Fort Drum.

"Danielle?" Justin had greeted her with the surprise of finding a good friend in an unexpected place. Danielle had liked Justin—even if he was a too-tall, too-handsome cowboy and completely knew it. But "good friend" was unusual for Danielle, with anyone, and Justin came close.

"Captain Roberts," as a dry greeting over the

top edge of her Suzanne Brockmann novel didn't faze him in the slightest.

"Mind if I join ya?" A question he then answered for himself by sliding into the opposite seat and taking a slice of her pizza. She been thinking of taking the leftovers back to base, but that was now an idle thought.

"Are you enjoying life in SOAR?" she did her best to appear a normal, social human, a skill she'd learned by rote. *Greeting someone you knew after a time apart? Ask a question about them.* "They treating you well?"

"Whoo-ee, you have no idea, Danielle," his voice was smooth as…well, always…so she wouldn't think about it also sounding like a pickup line. He was beautiful, but didn't interest her; the outgoing ones never did.

"Tell me." *Men love to talk about themselves, so let them.*

And he did. But she'd soon forgotten about her novel, and would have forgotten the pizza if he hadn't reminded her to eat.

His stories shifted from intriguing to fascinating. There was a world out there that she'd been only peripherally aware of. The Night Stalkers of the 160th SOAR weren't simply better helicopter pilots, they were the most highly-trained and best-equipped ones on the planet. Their missions were pure razor's edge and black-op dark.

He'd left her with a hundred questions and

enough interest to fill out an application to the 160th. Being a decent guy, Justin even paid for the pizza after eating half.

The speed at which she was rushed into testing told her that her meeting with Justin hadn't been by chance and that she owed him more than half a pizza next time they met. She'd asked after him a couple of times since she'd made it past the qualification exams—and the examiners' brutal interviews that had left her questioning her sanity, never mind her ability.

"Justin Roberts is presently deployed, ma'am," was the only response she'd gotten.

Now that she was through training—almost, had to be soon, didn't it?—Danielle realized that was probably less of an evasion and more likely to do with the brutal op tempo the Night Stalkers maintained. The SOAR 1st Battalion had just won the coveted Lt. General Ellis D. Parker awards for Outstanding Combat Aviation Battalion *and* Aviation Battalion of the Year. They'd been on deployment every single day of the last year, actually of the last decade-plus since 9/11.

The very first Special Forces boots on the ground in Afghanistan were delivered that October by the Night Stalkers and nothing had slacked off since. Justin might be in the 5th battalion D company, but they were just as heavily assigned as the 1st.

Part of their training had included tours in

Afghanistan. But unlike their prior deployments, these were brief, intense, and then they'd be back in the States pushing to integrate their new skills.

SOAR needed her training to end and so did she.

Danielle was ready for the job, in her own, inestimable opinion. But she wasn't going to get there until the trainers signed off that she'd reached fully mission-qualified proficiency.

The Fort Campbell training course was never set up the same from one flight to the next, but it always had a time limit. The time would be short and they didn't tell you what it was. So she drove the Chinook for all it was worth like Regina Jaquess waterskiing her way to U.S. Ski Team Female Athlete of the Year.

The Night Stalkers were a damned secretive lot, and after two years of training, she understood why. With seven years flying for the 10th, she'd thought she was good.

She'd been repeatedly lauded as one of the top pilots at Fort Drum.

The Night Stalkers had offered an education in what it really meant to fly. In the two years of her training, she'd flown more hours than in the seven years prior, despite two deployments to Iraq. And she'd spent more time in the classroom than her life-to-date accumulated flight hours.

But she was ready now. It was *très viscérale,* right down in her bones she could feel it. The

Chinook was as much a part of her nervous system as breathing.

Too bad they didn't build men the way they built the big Chinooks—especially the MH-47G which were built specifically to SOAR's requirements. The aircraft were steady, trustworthy, and the most immensely powerful helicopters deployed in the U.S. Army— what more could a girl ask for? But finding a superhero man to go with her superhero helicopter was just a fantasy for a lonely teenage girl.

She dove down into a canyon and slid to a hover mere inches over the reservoir inside the thirty-second window laid out on the flight plan.

Danielle resisted a sigh. She was ready for something to happen and to happen soon.

# # #

Pete's Chinook and his two escort Black Hawks crossed into the mountainous province of Sikkim, India ten feet over the glaciers and still moving fast. It was an hour before dawn, they'd made it out of China while it was still dark.

"Twenty minutes of fuel remaining," Nicolai said it like a personal challenge when they hit the border.

"Thanks, I never would have noticed."

It had been a nail-biting tradeoff: the more fuel he burned, the more easily he climbed due to the lighter load.

The more he climbed, the faster he burned what little fuel remained.

Safe in Indian airspace he climbed hard as Nicolai counted down the minutes remaining, burning fuel even faster than he had been while crossing the mountains of southern Tibet. They caught up with the U.S. Air Force HC-130P Combat King refueling tanker with only ten minutes of fuel left.

"Ram that bitch," Nicolai called out.

Pete extended the refueling probe which reached only a few feet beyond the forward edge of the rotor blade and drove at the basket trailing behind the tanker on its long hose.

He nailed it on the first try despite the fluky winds. Striking the valve in the basket with over four hundred pounds of pressure, a clamp snapped over the refueling probe and Jet A fuel shot into his tanks.

His helo had the least fuel due to having the most men aboard, so he was first in line. His Number Two picked up the second refueling basket trailing off the other wing of the Combat King. Thirty seconds and three hundred gallons later and he was breathing much more easily.

"Ah," Nicolai sighed. "It is better than the sex," his thick Russian accent only ever surfaced in this moment or while picking up women.

"Hey, Nicolai," Nicky the Greek called over

the intercom from his crew chief position seated behind Pete. "Do you make love in Russian?"

A question Pete had always been careful to avoid.

"For you, I make special exception." That got a laugh over the system.

Which explained why Pete always kept his mouth shut at this moment.

"The ladies, Nicolai? What about the ladies?" Alfie the portside gunner asked.

"Ah," he sighed happily as he signaled that the other choppers had finished their refueling and formed up to either side, "the ladies love the Russian. They don't need to know I grew up in Maryland and I learn my great-great-grandfather's native tongue at the University called Virginia."

He sounded so pleased that Pete wished he'd done the same rather than study Japanese and Mandarin.

Another two hours of—thank god—straight-and-level flight at altitude through the breaking dawn and they landed on the aircraft carrier awaiting them in the Bay of Bengal. India had agreed to turn a blind eye as long as the Americans never actually touched their soil.

Once standing on the deck—and the worst of the kinks had been worked out—he pulled his team together: six pilots and seven crew chiefs.

"Honor to serve!" He saluted them sharply.

"Hell yeah!" They shouted in response and

saluted in turn. It was their version of spiking the football in the end zone.

A petty officer in a bright green vest appeared at his elbow, "Follow me please, sir." He pointed toward the Navy-gray command structure that towered above the carrier's deck. The Commodore of the entire carrier group was waiting for him just outside the entrance. Not a good idea to keep a One-Star waiting, so he waved at the team.

"See you in the mess for dinner," he shouted to the crew over the noise of an F-18 Hornet fighter jet trapping on the #2 wire. After two days of surviving on MREs while squatting on the Tibetan tundra, he was ready for a steak, a burger, a mountain of pasta...maybe all three.

The green escorted him across the hazards of the busy flight deck. Pete had kept his helmet on to buffer the noise, but even at that he winced as another Hornet fired up and was flung aloft by the catapult.

"Orders, Major Napier," the Commodore handed him a folded sheet the moment he arrived. "Hate to lose you."

The Commodore saluted, which Pete automatically returned before looking down at the sheet of paper in his hands. The man left before the import of Pete's orders slammed in.

A different green-clad deckhand showed up with Pete's duffle bag and began guiding him toward a loading C-2 Greyhound twin-prop airplane. It was parked number two for the launch catapult, close behind the raised jet-blast deflector.

His crew, being led across in the opposite direction to return to the berthing decks below, looked at him aghast.

"Stateside," was all he managed to gasp out as they passed.

A stream of foul cursing followed him from behind. Their crew was tight. Why the hell was Command breaking it up?

And what in the name of fuck-all had he done to deserve this?

He glanced at the orders again as he stumbled up the Greyhound's rear ramp and crash landed into a seat.

Training rookies?

It was worse than a demotion.

This was punishment.

Target of the Heart *and other titles are available at fine retailers everywhere.*

Other works by M.L. Buchman

Cookbook from Hell: Reheated
Saviors 101

Don't Miss a Thing!
Sign up for M. L. Buchman's newsletter
today
and receive:
Release News
Free Short Stories
a Free Starter Library

Do it today. Do it now.
http://www.mlbuchman.com/newsletter/

Printed in Great Britain
by Amazon